KIDS HAVE FEELINGS, TOO SERIES

Moving Is Hard

By Joan Singleton Prestine
Illustrations by Virginia Kylberg

Fearon Teacher Aids

Editor: Susan Eddy

This Fearon Teacher Aids product was formerly manufactured and distributed by American Teaching Aids, Inc., a subsidiary of Silver Burdett Ginn, and is now manufactured and distributed by Frank Schaffer Publications, Inc. FEARON, FEARON TEACHER AIDS and the FEARON balloon logo are marks used under license from Simon & Schuster, Inc.

© Fearon Teacher Aids
A Division of Frank Schaffer Publications, Inc.
23740 Hawthorne Boulevard
Torrance, CA 90505-5927

ISBN 1-56417-676-2

1 2 3 4 5 6 7 8 9 SP 01 00 99 98 97

We've lived here for a long time. In this house. In this neighborhood. I like it here.

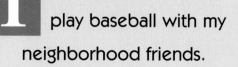

I play baseball with my neighborhood friends.

S cott and Debbie and Jeff and I trade books at the bus stop.

Buckles and I run in the fields.

I climb tall trees and spy on my whole world.

But now we are moving. I don't want to move. All my friends live here. I like this house and this neighborhood and I especially like my room.

Moving is hard. Our new house isn't a house. It's an apartment. And this neighborhood isn't a neighborhood. It's busy streets and tall buildings. There's no place to play baseball. I'll never use my mitt again.

I don't ride the school bus. There is no school bus. And I don't have any friends. I'll never trade books again.

There aren't any fields where Buckles and I can run. We'll never run together again.

There aren't any tall trees. There are only little baby trees. I'll never spy on my whole world again. Even though I didn't want to, we moved anyway.

Then I found out there's a baseball league. Now I play first base.

I carpool to school with Tonya and José.
We're friends and we trade books in the car.

I even found a park. Buckles
and I can run and run.

The best thing I found was a secret stairway that leads to the roof of my apartment building. I can spy on my whole world.

And my new room
is even better than my old one.

Even though I didn't want to move, we had to. I haven't lived here long. But I've decided that this apartment is a lot like my old house—only different. And these streets and buildings are a lot like my old neighborhood—only different. Even though moving is hard, I like it here. In my new apartment house. In my new neighborhood.

RED HOT
HOT DOGS

Discussing **Moving Is Hard** With Children

After reading the story, encourage discussion. Children learn from sharing their thoughts and feelings.

Discussion Questions for **Moving Is Hard**

- How did the girl feel about her new home when she first moved in? What did she miss? What was different?

- What did the girl do first when she moved into her new home? What would be the first thing you would do?

- How did her feelings change after she'd lived there for a while? What made them change?

- At the end of the story, what did she like about her new home?

Significance of **Moving Is Hard** for Children

Sometimes a book will trigger strong feelings in young children, especially if they have experienced similar situations. If they feel comfortable, encourage children to share their experiences. **Helping Children Cope With Moving** is a resource guide for **Moving Is Hard**. The guide is for adults to use with children. It includes suggestions for talking about moving, describes how children respond to their feelings, and offers several hands-on projects that may help children adjust to their new environments.